WE STAND UP FOR WHAT'S RIGHT

By Hassan El-Tayyab and Audra Caravas
Illustrated by Angelyca Moffatt

Poetic Matrix Press

WE STAND UP FOR WHAT'S RIGHT

Once upon a time or really today,

a village full of animals had a leader they say.

King Lion could decide on things they could do.

Which games they could play, which lands they could travel to.

One day King Lion demanded the
animals throw stones,

at some hungry neighbors who
stole a bone.

King Lion roared
loud after the
fight was won.

"Our foes are defeated and are now on the run."

But as the dust settled the animals looked all around.

They saw bumps and bruises, sad faces and frowns.

"Where's my mama?" one Little Lamb said.

Look over there she's got a bump on her head!

Everyone was crying and everyone felt sad.

Asking, "Why do we fight
when it feels so bad?"

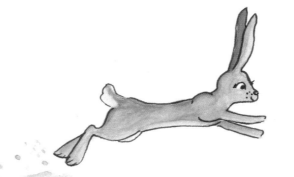

The whole town agreed to meet under the moon,

to discuss how they felt and what they would do.

Mrs. Fox stood up, raised her hand and said,

"We must answer some questions before we go to bed."

Why should we fight? Why should we fight?

Why does one person get to say if it's right?

Why should we fight? Why should we fight?

Shouldn't we ALL decide if it's wrong or it's right?

They conversed and debated and decided they must,
take this power from the King who they no longer did trust.

This angered King Lion and he roared, "I AM MAD!"

He demanded the power back that he once had.

But the animals stayed strong
and all spoke in one voice,

to say again loudly, "IT'S ALL OF OUR CHOICE!"

We all make the decision the Little Lamb did say,

whether we should vote yes or we should vote nay.

Lion huffed and puffed but eventually agreed.

Now they all live together in peace and harmony.

When the Little Lamb got older she ran for President and won.

Her winning campaign slogan was, "Less fighting, more love!"

Hassan El-Tayyab is an award winning songwriter, author, and the Friends Committee on National Legislation's lead lobbyist on Middle East policy. Hassan's passion for foreign affairs is rooted in his desire to make life better for people in the Middle East, including his extended family in Jordan. He is convinced that advancing a more peaceful and diplomacy-based foreign policy in the Middle East is critical, not only for the family he loves, but for peace and stability worldwide. His writings and commentaries have been featured in numerous news outlets, including The Hill, The Young Turks, Truthout, Al Jazeera, and more.

Audra Caravas graduated from in the University of Colorado in Boulder in which she helped develop a class called, "Democracy as a Tool for Social Change." She worked for the Colorado House of Representatives in which she wrote and published her first book, "I Can Make a Difference," a children's book that teaches how a bill becomes a law. In 2012 she ran for the Berkeley Rent Stabilization Board while earning her Master's Degree in Public Policy from Mills College. She has worked for various non-profit organizations including Greenpeace, Peace Action West, Clean Water Action, Girls Inc, Young Americans Center for Financial Education, Peace Village, and Democratic Direct a Political Consulting Firm in San Francisco. She believes that the love of our children is a love that binds us. Together we'll find the solutions we need to survive and thrive.